Diversity is You and Me

Written by
Jackie Scott-Bell

Text and illustration copyright 2020 by Scott Bell Management, LLC

scottbellmanagement@gmail.com

First edition

ISBN: 978-1-09832-758-3

To Jasmine and Jalen, the inspiration for everything I do

-Jackie

D is for each different face
that has its own shaped nose.

I is for the interests we share, like skating or wearing the same type of clothes.

V is for the variety of languages
that we hear people speak.

E is for everybody can make a difference,
it starts with you and me.

R is for the respect that each person deserves.

S is for saying nice and friendly words.

I is for identifying the uniqueness
of one another.

T is for taking time to listen
and learn about each other.

Y is for you and all the people
who make up the world universally.

Just like the letters that come together
and spell DIVERSITY.

**When we celebrate the beauty
of all the languages, ethnicities and colors...**

It helps us understand how we depend on each other.

Everyone benefits from worldwide contributions.

**Although we may not always agree,
we can work out a solution.**

**Appreciate the differences
in the people that you see.**

Diversity is what makes up the many cultures of people like you and me.

Glossary

Appreciate- know about and understand the value of someone

Celebrate- doing something special to recognize something important

Contribution- to join others in doing things to help

Culture- shared customs and traditions of a group of people

Diversity- a range of different people or things

Ethnicity- belonging to a group of people who share the same language, religion and customs

Identity- characteristics that make a person different from others

Respect- to treat others the way you would like to be treated

Solution- an answer to a question or problem

Unique- being the only one of its kind

Universal- including everybody and everything